This Walker book belongs to:

_____

FOR BEA

First published 2021 by Walker Books Ltd, 87 Vauxhall Walk, London SE11 5HJ

This edition published 2022

2 4 6 8 10 9 7 5 3 1

Printed in China

British Library Cataloguing in Publication Data: a catalogue record for this book is available
from the British Library

ISBN 978-1-5295-0423-1
www.walker.co.uk

WALKER BOOKS

AND SUBSIDIARIES

LONDON • BOSTON • SYDNEY • AUCKLAND

MIX
Paper from
responsible sources
FSC® C144853

IT'S MINE!

EMMA YARLETT

One day there was a thing.
Nobody knew how it had got there.

It just was.

Mouse was feeling hungry.
Mouse saw the thing.

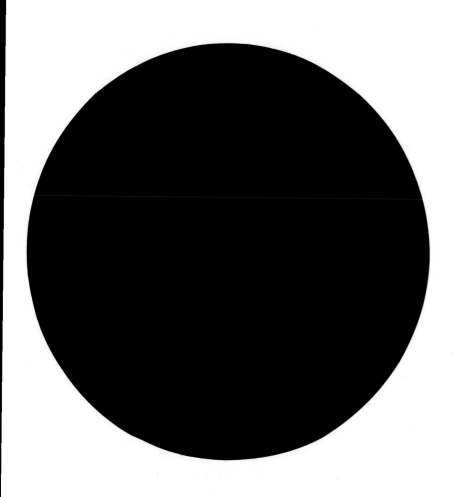

"TASTY FRUIT!"
said mouse.

" That fruit," said mou

" is mighty fine."

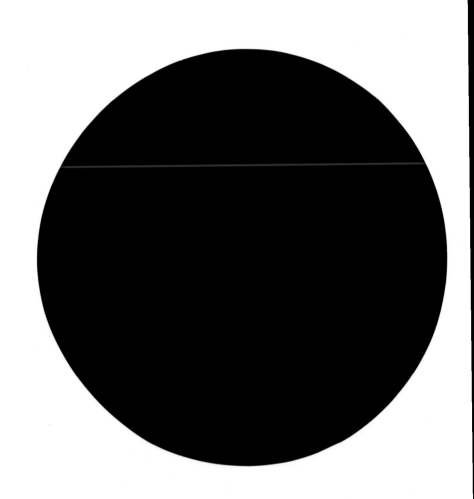

Frog needed a new wheel.
Frog saw the thing.

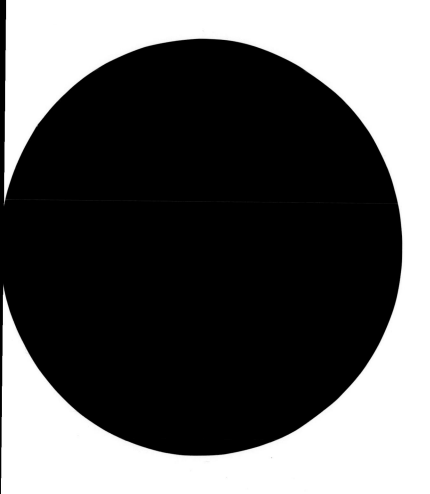

"Mouse has the
PERFECT WHEEL!"
said Frog.

"That wheel," said Fro

"is mighty fine."

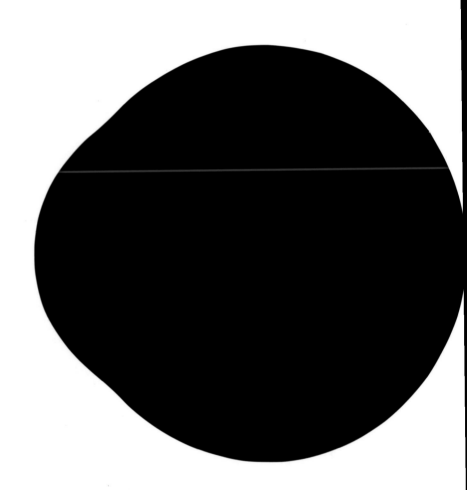

"That wheel," said Frog, "is mine, all MINE!"

Fox needed a new ball.
Fox saw the thing.

"That ball," said FOX, "is mine, all MINE!"

Bear needed a new chair.
Bear saw the thing.

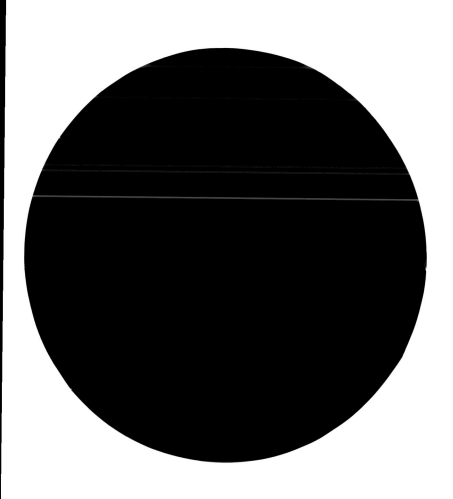

"Fox has the
PERFECT CHAIR!"
said Bear.

"That chair," said Bea
"is mighty fine."

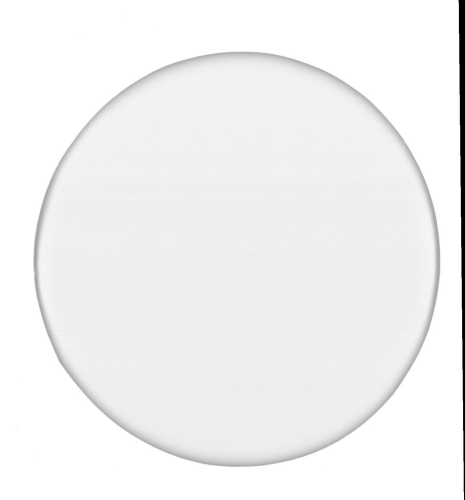

"That chair," said Bear,

Bear was enjoying her chair when...
"It's MINE!" said Mouse.
"It's MINE!" said Frog.
"It's MINE!" said Fox.
"It's MINE!" said Bear.

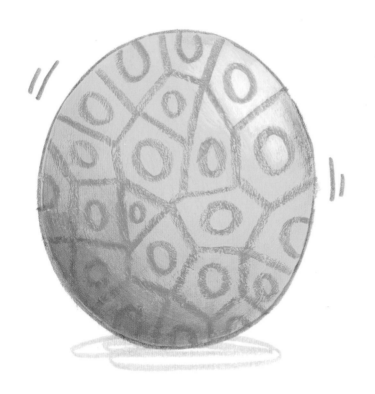

When all of a sudden there was a wobble,

a crack ...

a crunch ...

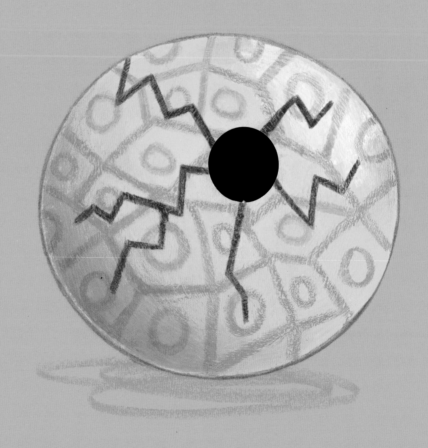

and a ...

"mine, all MINE!"
said Mama Crocodile.

And so it was.

Other books by Emma Yarlett

ISBN: 978-1-4063-7971-6

ISBN: 978-1-4063-8663-9

ISBN: 978-1-4063-9219-7

Available from all good booksellers

www.walker.co.uk